King Arthur
and the
Mighty Contest

Tony M

Illustr

ORCHARD BOOKS

CRAZY CAMELOT

MEET THE KNIGHTS OF THE ROUND TABLE:

King Arthur
with his sword so bright,

Sir Percival,
a wily knight.

Sir Kay,
a chap whose hopes are high,

Sir Lancelot,
makes ladies sigh.

Sir Gawain,
feeling rather green,

Sir Galahad,
so young and keen.

Sir Ack,
who's fond of eating lots,

Sir Mordred,
hatching horrid plots.

Morgana,
Arthur's wicked
sister,

Merlin.
That's me,
your wizard mister!

*To Sir Ralph of Bradmore Park,
valiant knight, from Tony Mitton,
Scribe to the Wizard Merlin*

*To Sir Hayden Thomas Skerry,
from Arthur Robins*

WORCESTERSHIRE COUNTY COUNCIL	
753	
Bertrams	26.03.06
	£3.99

ORCHARD BOOKS
96 Leonard Street, London EC2A 4XD
Orchard Books Australia
32/45-51 Huntley Street, Alexandria, NSW 2015
First published in Great Britain in 2003
First paperback edition 2004
Text © Tony Mitton 2003
Illustrations © Arthur Robins 2003
The rights of Tony Mitton to be identified as the author
and Arthur Robins as the illustrator of this work
have been asserted by them in accordance with the
Copyright, Designs, and Patents Act, 1988.
A CIP catalogue record for this book is available
from the British Library.
ISBN 1 84121 712 3 (hardback)
ISBN 1 84121 714 X (paperback)
1 3 5 7 9 10 8 6 4 2 (hardback)
1 3 5 7 9 10 8 6 4 2 (paperback)
Printed in Great Britain

In the days of Merrie England
when men wore stretchy tights,
the crazy castle Camelot
stood crammed with nutty knights.

They all sat round a table
dressed up in metal kit.
Their table was a round one
'cos a square one wouldn't fit.

They went on many adventures,
yes, they travelled wide and far.
They had to go by horse, of course,
as they hadn't got a car.

But in those days so long ago
it was easier to be brave.
There were loads of trolls and dragons,
and many maids to save.

So let me take a good old gulp
from my magic story cup.
And now let's spin the table
to see which knight pops up...

Before us stands King Arthur.
Of kings he was the best.
He knew no fear. He liked his beer,
and wore a metal vest.

I'll tell you the wondrous story
of how he came to rule.
So just stay put and listen.
It's crazy, but it's cool...

Under the old king, Uther,
everything seemed all right.
But somebody poisoned his porridge.
Then everyone started to fight.

Everyone wanted his castle.

Everyone wanted his crown.

But every time somebody grabbed them,

someone else knocked 'em down.

The nastiest knights went picking fights.
Bold barons unfurled their banners.
Everyone scrabbled for wealth and power,
and they all forgot their manners.

The country was seething with villains,
doing their pillage and loot.
There just wasn't anyone left in charge
to give them a good, strong boot.

Now, deep in the woods was a wizard,
a maker of mystery.
He could change himself into a bat
   (or a bird)
and hide in the boughs of a tree.

He was tall and thin and ancient,
with a beard and a brilliant cloak.
And the folk all called him Merlin,
that weird old wizard bloke.

But they knew he was really brainy.
Of that there could be no doubt.
So everyone hoped that Merlin
would sort this king-thing out.

And out from the wood he came at last,
wearing a serious frown.
He muttered a word, changed into a bird
and flew to London town.

In London he shook off his feathers
and summoned all knights and lords.
They came from all parts,
  hope high in their hearts,
with their helmets and shields and swords.

18

They scrapped and they yapped
    and they squabbled
like a pack of dogs with a bone.
For each great lump thought his
    very own rump
would comfortably fit the throne.

But, when they turned up at the meeting…
Blimey! What's this they found?!
A sword stuck into a boulder
had kind of *appeared* on the ground.

The boulder, it stood on a marble block.
On the block were words in gold:

Whoever can pull this sword out
gets the jackpot ~ it's his to hold!

But, more than that, the lucky old chap
who draws it out by hand,
why, that's the chap to cheer and clap
as King of all the land.

Well, everyone wanted to try their luck.
They queued from first to last.
But no one could budge that blade an inch.
The sword stuck firmly fast.

Many a knight came striding up
to hoik and heave and huff.
But every one went tottering back
all pale and out of puff.

So, in the end, they cried, "Enough!
This is a barmy test.
Let's put together a tournament
to see who jousts the best."

One of the knights, Sir Ector,
had brought his son, Sir Kay.
And Kay's young brother, Arthur,
was acting squire that day.

(A squire is a knight in training
who follows an older knight.
He works as a kind of servant
until he can get things right.)

Poor young Arthur was only a lad,
and, although he was brave and bold,
he had to follow his brother around
and do as he was told.

Just as they reached the tournament,
Kay cried out loud, "Oh Lord!"

Oh, blimey, golly!
I'm a wally!
I forgot me
sword!

So brother Arthur hurried back
to fetch it from their tent.
But the only sword that he could see
was blunt, and badly bent.

He went to seek some other sword,
he hunted all around...
until at last he came right past
that boulder on the ground.

He hadn't been old enough to join
the great big, grown-up knights.
He'd spent the day preparing Kay's
equipment for the fights.

So Arthur hadn't heard about
the boulder and its sword.
He simply guessed it had been left
by some forgetful lord.

And when he saw the trusty weapon
sticking in the air,
he reached straight out and gave a shout,
"I'll borrow that one there!

"I wouldn't dream of stealing it,"
he said. "It's just a loan."
Then, when he pulled, well,
    blow me down...
the blade slid out the stone.

So back he went to the tournament
and handed it to Kay.
But when his brother saw it,
his colour drained away.

"Crikey!" breathed the knight, in awe.
"Well, here's a sword to swing.
This very day the great Sir Kay
is destined to be king!"

Up strode Sir Ector, looking cross,
and gave his son a clout.
"You did your best and failed the test.
So put it back, you lout.

"If you can pull it out yourself,
just show me one repeat.
If you're My Lord, I'll eat my sword…
I'll even kiss your feet!"

Back they went to the boulder,
to try the test again.
But, try as he might, Sir Kay the knight
just tugged and tugged in vain.

"How did you do it, Arthur?"
he said with an angry hiss.
Arthur just reached his hand out.
"No sweat," he said. "Like this."

He lifted out the shining sword
and held it up aloft.
Sir Kay and old Sir Ector
both felt their knees go soft.

Sir Kay got slightly grumpy.
He sulked,

That can't be fair.
I'm the elder brother,
so I should be the heir.

"Not so," said old Sir Ector.
"For Arthur's not my lad.
I raised him as a foster son.
King Uther was his dad."

Well, soon the others gathered round
for rumours travel quickly.
"What, take this little wimp as king?"
they cried. "He's small and sickly!

"It isn't right. He's not a knight.
Besides, he's under age.
A lad like that, he's just a brat -
not fit to be a page."

But suddenly a shadow spread
as clouds blocked out the sun.
And Merlin the magician's voice
boomed,

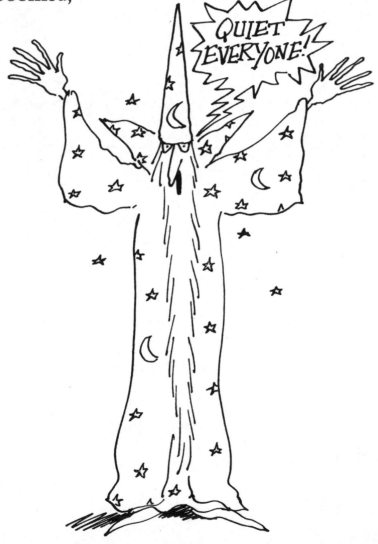

"I tell you all, my fortune ball
is glowing, and it shows…
it's crystal clear that this boy here's
the one the boulder chose.

"Sir Ector, here, has reared the lad
to be a worthy knight.
Swear on your swords, you other lords,
to serve him as is right."

The other knights knelt, muttering,
for Merlin was a wiz.
They knew too well he had a spell
to turn them into fizz.

They swore to serve King Arthur,
to be his faithful knights,
to keep their armour shining
and darn their holey tights.

Then Arthur stood and cleared his throat.
He felt all flushed and shy.
So he tried to make his voice sound deep,
though really it was high.

"We'll build a swanky castle.
We'll give it all we've got.
We'll fill it full of funky folk
and call it Camelot.

"We won't just hang out partying,
or feeling fat and bored.
We'll prove we're knights by finding fights
with lance and shield and sword.

"We'll take on trolls and dragons,
and chase big giants away.
Cool Camelot will be so hot,
and I'm the king - hooray!

"Then, when we're tired and hungry,
we'll meet back there for fun.
We'll sizzle pigs, do silly jigs -
and I'll be Number One!"

OK, that's it for now, from me,
your wizard story-teller.
But tune back in, for soon I'll spin
some other courtly fella.

CRAZY CAMELOT CAPERS

Written by Tony Mitton
Illustrated by Arthur Robins

Crazy Camelot Capers are available from all good bookshops,
or can be ordered direct from the publisher:
Orchard Books, PO BOX 29, Douglas IM99 1BQ
Credit card orders please telephone 01624 836000
or fax 01624 837033
or e-mail: bookshop@enterprise.net for details.

To order please quote title, author and ISBN
and your full name and address.
Cheques and postal orders should be
made payable to 'Bookpost plc'.
Postage and packing is FREE within the UK
(overseas customers should add £1.00 per book).

Prices and availability are subject to change.